Isn't She Lovely

Clairesville Series
Book 2.5

Nicole Mikell

P. Hollow Press

Copyright © 2026 by Nicole Mikell

All rights reserved.

No part of this book may be reproduced in any form or by any electronic or mechanical means, including information storage and retrieval systems, without written permission from the author, except for the use of brief quotations in a book review.

This is a work of fiction. Names, characters, places, and incidents either are the product of the author's imagination or are used fictitiously. Any resemblance to actual persons, living or dead, events, or locales is entirely coincidental.

First edition

ISBN: 979-8-9992297-2-4

Editor: Heather Epure

Cover Design: Gowtham T

For anyone that has ever struggled with their journey about motherhood...
This one is for you.

The wound is the place where the light enters you.

— Rumi

Music Playlist

This is the scannable code that goes along with the songs in each chapter!

It is in order so if you don't shuffle, you can just follow as the book goes.

Preface

This novella takes place after book 2 in the Clairesville series. If you have not read Baby, It's You and You Can't Hurry Love, I suggest doing so before you proceed with the story because you WILL be confused and there WILL be spoilers.
XO,
Nicole

Chapter 1

"We Made You"
Olive

"You're up, Hot Dog," Ivy shouts at Hunter from across the counter as I watch one of our regulars in a neon pink dress drunkenly step off the stage with Wes's assistance.

Hunter glances at me wide-eyed from behind a stack of glasses to my left. "I don't want to," he states. "I'm a different person than I was when I put my name on the list."

"Oh really?" I snort. "A different man than you were..." I look at the wall clock. "Twenty minutes ago?"

Turning back to the counter, I shake the cocktail mixer in my hands for a final time before pouring the dirty martini into a glass and setting it in front of Ivy.

She raises her eyebrow at me and wiggles her index finger. "He's not getting out of this."

"Oh, I know," I say with a grin. "It's my favorite part of the night."

"Agreed. Who knew your husband had such a talent when it came to rapping?"

"I mean, me." I laugh. "He's good with his tongue."

"I'm actually going to barf," Ivy teases. "I don't want to hear about Mom and Dad's sex life. It's like learning that there are bugs in chocolate; just let me enjoy you guys without the 'how it's made' part."

"We aren't your parents," Hunter answers. "But we *are* cutting you off after that cocktail."

"This isn't even your bar, so technically I don't have to listen to you, Hot Dog," she says flipping her long hair over her shoulder. "And don't worry, I'm getting a ride. Donovan will be heading into town any minute to get me."

"Oh, so in two hours?" Hunter jokes back.

Ivy's response is a drunken hiccup.

"He already texted me that he's almost here," I say to Hunter and then turn back to Ivy. "We *are* cutting you off after this," I tell her and blow an air kiss in her direction. "Love you, but it's for your own good. Tomorrow you will thank me."

"Fine." Ivy slumps farther down onto the barstool and angles her head slowly to my left to look at Hunter. "Now, go!"

"She'll never stop until you do." I look at my husband and lean in as I whisper into his right ear, "And... it kind of turns me on."

His eyes crinkle in response. "Fine. Can we do that thing later that I like if I do it?"

"Depends how well you do on stage," I smirk. "Now, get up there, Curls. Show me the reason why I married you."

"You didn't even know about this talent back then." Hunter smiles down at me, his eyes crinkling in the corners.

"You're right! And I might have married you even sooner if I did," I jokingly add. "I also expect you to do the chorus too, of course. No skipping out on the female vocals."

"Naturally. I know that's your favorite part." Hunter takes a deep breath, and I watch his floppy curls fall around his face in resolve as he steps around the side of the bar top.

A cheer rings out through the bar as he makes it up to the microphone and glances down at Wes, who's controlling the karaoke equipment.

"My usual," Hunter says to him, a tad reluctantly, and the patrons at the high tops and tables go wild.

The beat of the Eminem song begins to play throughout the speakers, and I cover my mouth with my hands, suppressing a laugh, as I watch Hunter take a deep breath to get in the zone. He begins to sing the intro female vocals loudly into the microphone, and I share a look with Ivy.

"This made my night!" She shouts to me and begins swaying along to the song, mouthing the lyrics slightly offbeat from her drunken stupor. I glance back at my husband, unable to bite back my grin.

Who would have thought that the man who was shy about getting up on stage that first night we met here, would now be making a fool of himself in a packed room on a Tuesday night—just for the hell of it.

Wes hops up onto the stage next to Hunter, and I roll my eyes as he starts pretending to make out with the side of Hunter's head. I think it physically pains Wes to not get all of the attention for more than one minute. We still love him though; he's like a dog that isn't fully house trained. He's harmless, and you love him, but at some point you're like... come on now, you have to stop humping my husband's leg.

The likelihood of Wes ever settling down like the rest of us someday is comical. The women in our group constantly give him shit about his Peter Pan Syndrome. The expression "when pigs fly" comes to mind whenever he mentions that someday he will commit to a woman.

"He really is an idiot." Ivy laughs, still facing the stage.

"Thank god you didn't end up with him," I tell her over the

music. "I think both of you would have spent more time looking in the mirror than at each other."

She whips around on the stool to face me again. "Only you can get away with saying that," Ivy snaps. "And it's because I know you're right, you sarcastic bitch."

"Let's all say thank god for Donovan," I tease her.

"Thank god for Donovan," we both say in unison.

"Did someone summon me?" Donovan asks, pushing through a few dancing couples gently to make his way over to Ivy. "Geez, it's a damn maze in here tonight."

"Baby!" She hops up from her barstool and into his arms.

"Woah." Donovan chuckles and stops her from stumbling over. "Been drinking a little this evening, have you, babe?" He looks down at her and gives her a knowing smile.

"I had to celebrate," Ivy shrieks over the music. "I sold my five thousandth dress today! And listen, I only thought it would be four thousand and ninety-nine today, but then the bride bought two!"

"Wow." Donovan grins and holds his arms around her lovingly. "That's amazing, Ivy."

"You two are so fucking cute," I say with a sigh, setting my arms against the counter. "When the hell are you guys going to get married?"

"Oh!" Ivy's eyes light up. "We—"

Donovan quickly cuts her off. "Babe, are you ready to go home and lie down? You're looking a little green."

They seem to share a silent conversation back and forth with their eyes, and then I watch as Ivy's grows super wide, as if she just realized something.

"Yes, yes. I'm sick. So sick," she hurriedly states and steps out of Donovan's hold. I watch, confused, as she runs around the bar and gives me a hug goodbye. "Love you! I'll text you tomorrow."

Donovan tries to hand me his card to pay for Ivy's tab, but I quickly shake my head "no." "Absolutely not. You just get her home. I'll never take your money here." I motion towards Ivy, who's starting to make her way through the crowd. "Like she said, tonight was a night of celebrating."

Donovan's dark eyes illuminate with kindness. "Thank you. We will see you at the lake next weekend, right?"

"Of course, I can't wait to try and ski... This time, I think I can do it."

"You can," Hunter responds confidently, grabbing my hips as he steps behind me again. I didn't even notice he was done on stage.

"I agree with Hunter," Donovan answers, looking stressed as he realizes that Ivy is long gone. "I've got to go." He rushes off, and Hunter and I share a laugh.

"Great performance, by the way," I say, turning around to face him.

"Thank you." Hunter smiles and leans down closer to my ear. "So, what you're saying is we can do that thing tonight?"

"Yes," I respond, "we can do *that* thing."

Chapter 2

"Obsessed With You"
Hunter

"**F**aster!" Olive groans. "I'm almost there!"

I look over at my wife, who's sitting in a tee shirt of mine that is completely oversized on her and a pair of my boxer briefs. She's almost falling off the couch because she's so invested in the racing video game, and I can't help but mess with her.

"God, you're competitive," I tease her. "You know I'm going to win."

"Not a chance, I've been practicing." She rapidly pushes down on the buttons extra hard as if it will make her red Corvette go faster on the screen.

"No, you haven't!" I throw my head back and laugh as I watch her mash the X and B controls repeatedly with her thumbs. "When?"

"I swear!" Olive shrieks next to me, and I watch as her car slams into the side of the bridge on the racetrack. "Shit, never mind." She chucks the controller onto the couch with a huff.

My car crosses the finish line seconds later, and "victory" is plastered across the screen in metallic letters.

Olive groans. "I really *have* been practicing, though. I played while you were doing the Mathews' wedding last week for four hours straight, and I won almost every race." She crosses her arms. "One of these days, I'm going to smoke you."

I lean across the couch and grab her ankle out from under her, pulling her onto her back before I slowly crawl over her.

"Oh yeah?" I whisper. "You are?"

"You can count it," she says, pretending to pout as I lean down and start kissing her neck slowly.

A moan escapes her lips—my favorite sound–and I nip slowly at her collarbone with my teeth.

"Winner picks first?" I ask her, still moving my teeth against her soft skin.

An answering breathless moan from her lips gives me confirmation.

I slowly inch down her body, peppering her with kisses until I reach her thighs and open her smooth legs slowly. It's like I am unwrapping my favorite gift, and no matter how many times I get the present, I still feel like the luckiest man on earth.

I leisurely pull down my briefs that she's wearing and watch as she lifts her hips, inviting me in. She has nothing on underneath; her pussy is perfectly exposed and waiting for me. I blow a slow breath against her bare skin and watch as she twitches gently.

This is my favorite part of video games.

Bending down, I spread her legs wider and my mouth waters as I get my first taste of her—a sweet, delicate taste that I've continually craved since the very first time I experienced it.

Olive cries as she wraps her legs up around my shoulders, and I smile as I bury my face between her legs before licking her clit up and down with my tongue.

"Who do you think will win this time?" I ask, drawing back from her. "Who's coming first?"

"Me." Olive pants, "I'm going to."

"You always are so good at winning this game, baby," I rasp out before leaning down to lick her sensitive skin again.

I feel my dick push against my pants so hard it almost pains me. I need to make love to her. I think I might go insane if I don't get to be inside her soon.

I spread her pussy with my fingers and dip my tongue inside her even further.

"Hunter," Olive moans out loudly, and I insert two fingers in her, feeling her insides clenching around me.

My dick is instantly jealous of my hand.

I watch with my fingers still inside of her as Olive breathes through the final waves of her orgasm. Once she stops convulsing around me, I remove my fingers from her slowly, and she opens her eyes to look up at me with a dazed expression.

Her usually pale skin is flushed from pleasure as I sit up from between her thighs, climbing my body back up towards her face.

She pants against my mouth as I rest less than an inch away from hers. "I love you so much."

"I love you," I tell her, and kiss her forehead tenderly.

She scoots to her side so I can spoon her on the couch, and she breathes out and relaxes in my hold. The sensation of holding her against my body is like two puzzle pieces clicking together—everything is exactly how it should be.

Olive rests her arms against mine, and we hold each other for a moment longer in the silence of our house as I look out the large glass window of our living room to the dark forest behind.

How did I ever get so lucky in this life?

I ask myself this multiple times a day. I have the career I've always dreamed of and the woman I could never even *consider* dreaming of. She surpasses my every expectation of what a partner should be.

Olive speaks up, drawing me from my thoughts. "Alright, now it's the loser's choice."

"What?" I ask, huffing out a laugh.

She turns around on the couch to face me. "You heard me, I lost the game. Now I get to pay up and I can tell my reward is already ready to go."

"It's fine if you're tired, babe," I tell her.

"Shhhh, I'm not." Olive slips her hand into my pants, touching my agonizingly hard dick. " It's my turn to make you feel good, Curls."

And damn, she does.

Chapter 3

"Growing Pains"

Olive

"How did you know you were ready?" I ask Johnny, sliding a burger with extra pepperjack cheese and two pickles in front of him.

"Ready for what?"

"To have kids."

Rick lets out a chuckle from the end of the table. We both glance at him, and he looks up from his newspaper, apologizing before glancing back down like nothing happening.

"I didn't really have a choice," Johnny replies. "I mean, I did have a choice because, ya know... I stuck it in," I cringe at his words as he continues to talk, "but I mean, it wasn't something we planned. We just did it and then bam—in nine months, had Hally."

"Yeah, got it. I know how it happens," I snort. "I just didn't know if there was some point where you woke up and were like 'Yes, I've got this,' and felt confident about it."

As Johnny throws his shiny bald head backwards laughing, I can't help to miss that top hat he used to wear everyday. I'm happy he's confident in himself now, but I can't help but to feel nostalgic about it.

"Oh, you'll never feel that way," Johnny says, wiping a tear from under his eye.

"Okay, it wasn't that funny," I say as I roll my eyes. "I just want to know if there's a right time."

"Nope," Rob comments as his head pops out from the kitchen window. "Just do it, and the time will change along with you. And do it soon if you are, because Missy and I would like a friend for Rainn."

"Yeah, yeah. I've heard the same thing from Summer, she's due any day now and she and Eddie are really putting the pressure on us."

"Well, don't do it just because someone else tells you to," Rick responds, placing his newspaper on the bar counter. "Make sure it's what you and Hunter actually want."

Tate walks out from the swinging kitchen door and hands me two slices of chocolate pie. "Who wants kids in this economy? That sounds like torture."

I walk the pie over to Johnny and place a slice in front of him before sliding the other one to Rick. Johnny slides his burger to the side and begins to dig into the dessert. I have half a mind to tease him and make a comment about him not spoiling his meal.

"Thanks, Tate." Rick grins. "I've had a major sweet tooth recently."

"No problem, Grandpa. It's on me," he responds, and I chuckle at the nickname.

Rick doesn't have any kids of his own, but Tate insists on calling him "grandpa" for some reason. He told me that Rick deserves the title because he's so fatherly, but the ironic thing is Rick has never had any desire to be a dad.

"I've always wanted kids... I think? I just don't feel like I can have them," I admit. "I don't think I would be a good mom."

Johnny drops the pie-covered fork that's halfway into his mouth down onto his plate with a loud clatter.

"Now why would you ever say something like that?" He pushes the pie to the side as if he's lost his appetite from my comment.

Rob responds from the window behind me saving me from the embarrassment of admitting the reason why.

"Because of her relationship with her own mom."

"Yes," I say quietly. If anyone knows the turmoil of my childhood, it's the people standing in the bar right now. I've known Rick, Johnny, and Rob since I was eighteen years old– they've known me from the second I got away from my birth mom, Laurie.

They know about all the trials and tribulations I've gone through with Laurie, the abandonment and constant parentification of our relationship. I spent more of my life without a parent that cared, than with one.

It messed me up. Hell, it *still* messes me up.

Rick snaps me out of my thoughts. "Olive, don't even think that way about yourself," he tells me. "If one day you choose that you want to be a parent, you will be a great one. Hunter as well. Any kid would be lucky to have you guys raise them."

"Things just feel messy." I look away to hide the emotion tightening my throat. "How can I ever be a mom when I don't even know what a mom is supposed to be?"

"What do you think a mom is supposed to be?" Rick asks, lifting a bite of pie to his mouth.

"Well..." I think for a moment. "I guess a mom is supposed to care for you. Also, love you unconditionally and provide support for you in all parts of your life."

"And you don't think you don't already do that for people?"

Rick raises an eyebrow and then nudges his head in the direction of Johnny.

Following his eyes, I watch as Johnny lifts his burger to his mouth, and a large glob of ketchup drops off the backside of the bun onto his white shirt. I reach under the counter to grab a stack of napkins then place them in front of him.

"Yeah," Johnny agrees, shaking his head. "I think you do it already, too! You're not only the owner of Whiskey Jane's, but the mom of it as well."

"Have you ever thought of trying to talk to your mom? Maybe get some closure?" Rick asks.

I haven't told Hunter or anyone this, for that matter, but I have been dreaming about Laurie constantly these past few weeks. I feel like there is something going on with her, but I'm too scared to go looking.

I don't want to open a door that I'll never be able to close again.

"Maybe," I quietly answer.

"Well," Johnny replies playfully. "The good thing about maybes is they usually are actually bullshit. You know what you're going to do one way or the other."

The room grows quiet, and the only sound is Rob clearing his throat before he pats the window frame and steps back into the kitchen.

"I've got to submit this liquor order before I forget," I utter to Rick and Johnny, changing the subject. "I'll be back in ten."

Without listening to them as they continue their conversation, I push through the swinging door to the kitchen and ponder over Johnny's words.

What scares me is I know he's right. From the first dream I had about her weeks ago, I felt like I have to go finally visit my birth mom.

Chapter 4

"Take Me to the Hospital"
Olive

The wind whips violently through my hair, and I scream as Leena and Ivy screech to my left while both holding onto the float for dear life. We are going so fast, I can hardly catch my breath.

The fact that I'm tubing next to my best friend who couldn't even think about going in the lake or any body of water less than two years ago is insane. Donovan really helped her to face her fears and grow as a woman. Ivy spends every chance she gets on the lake now.

Leena screams at the top of her lungs, "Slow down, Ezra; I'm going to have a heart attack, and then I'll haunt you from the grave for doing this to me."

The sound of Donovan, Parker, and Hunter laughing loudly comes from the boat fifty feet in front of us.

"No way!" Ezra shouts back. "You knew what you were getting into when you chose to ride on the tube with me steering."

I look down at my chest and see that my right boob is on the verge of popping out from the crazy ride. Ivy notices too and starts laughing manically as she shouts, "Slow down, Olive is about to lose her top."

That seems to get through to Ezra, and he substantially slows down before cutting off the engine of the boat so that we are just floating calmly on the lake.

"Thank god," Leena remarks.

"I almost peed myself," Ivy yelps from between us.

"Well, thank god again then, because I don't want to be covered in pee," Leena states, and I can't hold back my laughter as I fix my swimsuit top. Leena is the most unintentionally funny person I know.

"That was so fun," I say breathlessly. "Let's do it again."

"I'm engaged," Leena states like she's talking about the weather.

"What?" Ivy and I shout in unison. I feel like we have been here before.

"What do you mean, you're engaged?" I ask hurriedly.

"Since when?" Ivy adds, grabbing onto Leena's shoulders and shaking her.

Leena slowly takes Ivy's hands off her, and I stifle a laugh. "Calm down, small stuff," she tells Ivy. "It's going to be okay."

"When did this happen?" I shake my head in disbelief. "I thought you never wanted to get married?"

"I didn't... I still kinda don't, but this is the right thing. I've been with Parker forever, and he wants this." Leena shrugs, "And I want him."

I eye her a little skeptically. I don't want her committing to someone for the rest of her life just to appease him. No matter how much she might love Parker, marriage is a huge commitment. Every time I've ever talked to Leena about marriage in the past, she's made it very evident that settling down with a license isn't something she looks for in her future.

"Are you sure about this?" I ask softly, not wanting to make her feel bad or think that I'm judging her.

Leena looks at me, her expression serious. "I'm sure. I want to get married to Parker."

"Okay," I answer, trying to force a convincing smile.

"Okay," Leena repeats; her mind is obviously made up about this. If she's sure, I'm happy for her.

"Okay?" Ivy parrots while glancing between the two of us. "So..." Ivy claps her hands together. "Can we celebrate now?"

"No," Leena responds. "I haven't even picked out a ring."

"Got it," Ivy cheerly states. "So ring, and then planning, and then picking out your dress at Vera Bridal of course." Ivy clasps her hands together, and I can tell she's already mentally putting Leena in gowns from her store as she eyes her. "I've been waiting for this day... I already have about ten dresses that would look fab on you."

"It's going to be a long engagement. I already told Parker that we will be taking our time," Leena answers, before raising her eyebrows mischievously and turning the question back on Ivy. "And how about you? When are you and Donovan going to formally commit to each other?"

I swear I see Ivy pale for a second when she answers quickly, "We are *also* taking our time."

"There's nothing wrong with any of our timelines," I say. "As long as we are happy *most* of the time, cause I mean, who the fuck is happy literally all the time? Except you, Ivy, no one is as happy as you are at eight am. You're unnatural," I tease.

Ivy laughs at my remark and shimmies her chest, as Leena nods in agreement with me.

"But, anyways," I continue. "We are all right where we need to be in life."

"Leena!" Parker yells urgently from the boat in front of us.

"What?" she responds, sitting up from the tube quickly.

"Summer's water just broke! I just got off the phone with Eddie. They are headed to the hospital!"

"Holy shit! You're about to be an aunt," Ivy cheers and jumps up to hug Leena, almost flipping our tube over. "We all are!"

Looks like a new member of our group is ready to make their appearance, and they are about to be spoiled as hell.

Chapter 5

"Real Love Baby"

Hunter

Two weeks later

Pulling up in front of Eddie and Summer's house, I take in the massive display of green and yellow balloons that surrounds their front porch in an arch. Wow, someone went all out for the arrival of baby Kai.

I look down at the small bouquet of sunflowers and children's board book next to me in the passenger seat of my truck and suddenly feel my gift is inadequate. I should have thought of something better for them.

Before I can second-guess my purchase any longer, Eddie pops his head out the front door and gives me a big wave. I wave back and blow out a breath as I put my truck in park before getting out with the presents.

"I thought I heard your old truck!" Eddie laughs.

"Hey man," I respond. "Sorry if it's too loud. I hope I didn't wake Kai."

"Nonsense," Eddie tells me. "The only thing that wakes

Kai is the second that Summer tries to take a shower, or nap, or eat, or sit him down."

"Oh, so it's true what they say?" I chuckle.

"Yeah, no one sleeps—except sometimes Kai," Eddie says with a nod of his head.

Once I get closer to Eddie, I see that he has large bags under both eyes and they are completely bloodshot.

"How many hours are you averaging?" I question.

"About one and a half," Eddie smiles.

"That's no worse than college, right?" I joke.

"Right." Eddie snorts. "The only saving grace is that I love the little guy so much, and everything he does is cute, so I don't even care that I'm running on fumes."

"Everything?"

"Everything. I know it sounds like bullshit, but I mean it. Even their poops are cute, because they're like so tiny and have these funny little diapers that look like they belong on a teddy bear."

"Yeah, man, I think that sleep deprivation might be getting to you," I tease him.

"It's the best, dude. I swear." Eddie wraps his arm around my shoulder and leads me to their house. "I thought I loved Summer before, but man, seeing her do something like that... Incredible."

I shake my head in agreement, thinking about how it would feel to see Olive go through something like childbirth. It honestly scares me, but I know she would be so strong, like she always is about everything else in life.

Eddie pushes open their front door, and I'm instantly surrounded by vases of flowers, balloons, and stuffed animals that line the hallway.

"Watch your step." Eddie chuckles. "Our relatives have been going a little insane with the gifts."

"I see that," I say, raising my eyebrows. Now I feel extra guilty that I just bought the same old crap as everyone else.

Eddie leads me to their minimalist family room and I see Summer sitting on the couch with her long red hair balled up on top of her head and a tiny baby in her arms.

She looks up from Kai and grins. "Hi, Hunter. Come meet your little nephew."

Smiling at the term "nephew"—although we aren't actually family, Eddie has always been like my brother—I walk up slowly, scared to spook the little guy. I've never really been around babies before since I was an only child and didn't have any cousins growing up.

I set the flowers and board book down on the coffee table in front of her and say sheepishly, "Sorry the gift isn't anything special; I see other people had the same idea as me."

"You didn't have to get anything at all, I appreciate it though," Summer says with a yawn and then grins again. Although she also looks exhausted, she too carries the satisfied, loving expression on her face that Eddie has.

Stammering, I add, "Olive said to tell you she's sorry she can't be here," I glance down at baby Kai and then back at Summer. "She got called into Whiskey's, one of the barbacks called out sick."

Summer brushes it off. "Don't worry about it, I've already seen her four times this week and still have a casserole she made me that I haven't even eaten yet." Summer laughs. "She's done plenty."

I was a little bit surprised myself that Olive has been by their house so much. I know she loves her friend, but she's never really seemed that into holding babies before. Every time Eddie's had to leave their home for some reason, Olive comes over here to help Summer by cleaning the house or watching Kai so she can catch a short break of sleep between feedings.

I haven't been over to meet Kai yet because my mom said I should give Summer a bit of time to recover after giving birth. She also said that she doesn't need visitors unless they are helping while Summer's newly postpartum—I took her word about that.

"Go ahead, you can hold him," Eddie tells me as he sits down on the cream couch next to Summer.

"I don't know," I say, rubbing my hand anxiously across the back of my neck. "I don't want to hurt him."

"You won't," Summer tells me softly. "I have a feeling you're going to be a natural. Here, sit right there." She motions over to a chair near the couch.

The tone of her voice is so reassuring that I almost believe her. "Okay," I agree and sit down slowly. "What do I do?"

Eddie scoots forward and gently takes Kai from Summer's arms so she doesn't have to sit up before transferring him to me.

"Here," he tells me. "Put one arm under his head to support him, and cup your other arm under his body like this."

Eddie lowers him into my arms, and I feel my heart begin to beat faster. Nothing puts pressure on you like holding the most important thing that has ever been created by two people you love.

"It's okay," Summer says with a small chuckle. "You can breathe, Hunter."

"Okay," I whisper and exhale a slow breath.

"He likes when you talk to him," Eddie speaks up. "Tell him about yourself."

"Okay," I repeat and look down at Kai. He rests in my arms with his eyes open slightly, looking as perfect as a baby doll. He looks exactly like Eddie with a little bit of Summer mixed in. He has Eddie's brown eyes and tan skin and Summer's thick red hair across his tiny head.

"Well," I clear my throat and start to say, "I'm Hunter, your dad's fri—your uncle, I guess?" I chuckle and look up at Eddie and Summer, who are both nodding in encouragement. "I, uh, I'm married to a lovely woman named Olive; she's your aunt. I guess you know her," I stammer. "You actually probably know her a lot better than me because she's been over here quite a bit."

Summer laughs and interjects, "Thank god for that."

Kai looks up at me, and I continue to talk to him. "I've known your dad for a really long time, since we were kids actually, and although I haven't known your mom as long as your dad, I can tell you they are both really good people. You were born into the best family."

I see Eddie wrap his arm around Summer's shoulders out of the corner of my eye. I look up at them and smile. "You guys look like you just stepped out of a family portrait."

"Yeah, right." Summer snorts. "I wish... I feel like I'm not going to remember any of these early days. It all feels like such a blur when you're in the middle of it."

And that's when it comes to me, the perfect gift.

"Eddie," I say, looking up. "Can you take Kai so I can grab my camera out of the car? I'd love to take some photos and videos for you guys."

With that, Summer bursts into tears.

I glance at her, concerned. "We don't have to; it was just an idea."

"Sorry, sorry," she responds through tears and starts laughing. "I promise I'm not actually crying over anything serious. That just sounds amazing, and I'm sleep-deprived."

Eddie stands to take Kai from me and hands him over gently before saying, "One photoshoot from Rowe Records coming right up."

Chapter 6

"Stranger"
Olive

Pulling my SUV into the lot of the Jewel Mountain Motel, I look around at the depressing, rundown space. Nothing has changed after all these years; it still looks like a tornado ran through it and dropped the building back down after as a courtesy.

The last time I was here I was about thirteen years old, eating stale vending machine Cheetos, and sitting on the end of the motel bed listening to Laurie crying in the bathroom on the phone with my so-called "dad." It was one of many times that the police separated them for the night after yet another domestic dispute call.

This parking lot alone makes acidic bile rise in my throat without even stepping out of my vehicle. I have half a mind to put my car in reverse and leave, putting this all behind me. I take a deep breath and gather myself—if there's one thing I'm not, it's weak.

Reaching over onto the passenger seat, I grab a to-go box filled with a lunch wrap and fries that I had Rob make before he left for the night. I also bought a new set of clothes and a white envelope that I put fifty dollars in.

Taking a deep breath, I push open my driver's side door and get out fumbling with all the items in my hands. I step across overgrown weeds sprouting out of the sidewalk and walk up the concrete staircase to the second floor of the motel. A wave of nausea hits me as soon as I see the room number I'm looking for, 2218.

I'm instantly thankful that it's nighttime so I don't have to worry about anyone seeing me. I'm already shaking like a leaf, and my head is swimming with a newfound anxiety that I didn't think would happen. I thought I could handle this, but I feel my head spinning each step closer.

I think of Hunter's smile and tussling his curls to try and calm myself as I approach my destination.

Once I arrive in front of the door, I stare at the chipped brown paint with the worn letters. I can hear the sound of a TV playing a show loudly from inside.

She's here.

My stomach lurches, and I breathe through my nose slowly as I bend down and place the contents from my hands down onto the Jewel Mountain Motel mat in front of the doorway. There's an overflowing ashtray and a crumpled-up beer can next to my feet. I just need to get this over with before I faint.

Three... two... one... I tell myself, forcing my shaky legs to stand back up and knock on the door.

The solid sound of my knock reverberates down the concrete hallway, and I hear the muffled TV volume lower slightly.

Instantly I lose my nerve and sprint like an absolute maniac to the other side of the motel before ducking into an open doorway labeled "Laundry."

Breathing heavily, I peek out of the dark, vacant laundry

room and watch as the door opens slightly. I watch as an old, fragile-looking woman steps out of the room slowly and bends down to look at the items on the mat.

I almost gasp when I realize it is her; it's my mother, Laurie. She looks nothing like the woman I last saw all those years ago. She looks weak—at least twenty years older than she actually is—and her face looks like it's bruised on the left side.

More than anything else, she looks nothing like the striking woman that she once was. As much as I disliked Laurie, she was always beautiful. That's how she found men to love her so easily—no matter how toxic it was on both ends, they wanted her.

She grabs the items up from the mat and looks down one side of the walkway before glancing down the side where I'm hiding. I duck back into the dark room, praying that she didn't see me.

I can't do it tonight. I'm just not ready.

Chapter 7

"Heart Full of Soul"
Hunter

Olive walks up behind me at my desk and hugs the back of my neck. "I can't believe you're still awake," she says, her breath tickling against my skin.

I swivel around in my chair to face her and shrug. "I wanted to wait up for you."

She glances at the clock behind me on my computer monitor. "It's almost midnight," she comments.

"You're worth the wait. Always have been, always will be" I respond.

Olive leans forward and kisses me gently on the lips. Her hair smells faintly like alcohol and burger grease—I breathe in the smell of Whiskey Jane's.

"You always know how to make me feel beautiful when I'm covered in sweat and draft beers."

"You are beautiful," I whisper, squeezing her hand tenderly. She sits down on my lap and rolls her neck around in a circle to try and relieve tension from her day. "Sit in front of me," I tell her. "I'll massage it."

"Thank you," Olive replies and slides from my lap onto the floor in front of me.

I move her long, dark hair to the side and begin to massage the tight knots out of her neck with my hands.

Olive visibly relaxes as I work on the tense spots, and she lets out a groan of pleasure. "This was just what I needed."

"Rough night?"

"Kinda," she replies. "Just sort of a weird one, you could say."

"Want to talk about it?"

"Actually, I'd prefer a record instead, if that's okay?"

"You've got it," I say, standing from the chair and stepping around her. "What are you in the mood for?"

"Hmmm," she thinks for a moment before her eyes light up. "The Yardbirds."

"*Shapes of Things* or *For Your Love?*"

Olive shakes her head. "*Having a Rave Up with The Yardbirds.*"

"Good choice." I scan the wide shelf in my office for the album until I spot it. "Found it."

I set the record on the player and set the needle, watching as the disk begins to spin slowly and the album starts to play the soulful oldies rock and roll.

Sitting back behind Olive in the chair, I continue to rub her shoulders as we listen to track after track of the record. Eventually, I feel her body relax completely.

As I stop, she leans back up against me and whispers, "Thank you."

"You deserve it; you work so hard, babe." Olive slowly stretches out her legs in front of her as I sheepishly add, "I, on the other hand, had a pretty easy day."

"Oh my god, I feel like a bitch for not asking." She sits up quickly and turns to face me, her doe eyes wide with regret. "How was your day? How was meeting baby Kai?"

"Olive, don't worry about it." I reach forward and tussle her hair jokingly, like she has done to me for so many years.

She rolls her eyes and laughs. "Ha-ha, very funny. Now tell me."

"It was awesome." I can't hide my grin. "He's so cute and special. It's so cool to see how he's the perfect combination of both Eddie and Summer." I think about how Kai looked up at me, so enthralled with studying my face. "And he held onto my finger for like ten minutes straight." I hold up my hand and laugh. "It was crazy; his whole hand just fit around my index finger. Eddie says it means he likes me."

Olive looks at me for a long time, studying my obviously excited expression, but instead of agreeing with me like I thought she would, she almost looks somber.

"Are you okay?" I ask her.

"You want a baby, huh?" She replies, but it's so quiet, I almost can't hear her.

I shrug, not wanting to make her feel pressured. The truth is before today, I knew I wanted to have kids at some point, but after today, I feel like I need to have kids with her. A new spot has opened up in my heart, and I'm afraid only a child with Olive could fill it.

"I mean," I tell her. "I would love to have a child with you at some point, you know. But I would also understand if you don't want to have one. It's your body that has to go through everything; I just get to... you know... do the fun stuff to make it happen."

Olive snorts. "Yes, I know." She looks away and busies herself by picking at a spot of some kind of dried food from work that's stained on the knee of her pants.

I know Olive struggles with stuff like this because of her

upbringing. She tends to shut down when the children topic comes up.

"It's always up to you, I will never pressure you."

"And that's why I love you so much, because you're just you. You just understand without having to be told. Hell, you see me even when I don't even want to see myself."

She begins to stand up from the floor, and I take her hands, pulling her up the rest of the way.

Olive glances at the computer screen that's illuminated behind me and asks, "Were you editing something?"

I swivel around in my chair and face the screen, clicking open one of the tabs at the bottom of the monitor. "I took some photos of Eddie, Summer, and Kai today. Wanna see?"

"Of course," Olive responds, leaning down over the desk next to me.

I open up the editing software and begin to click through some of the photos of the happy family. Olive smiles at a few, making comments, and laughs when she sees the ones I took right when Kai sneezed.

Clicking to the next photo, I suddenly see myself on the screen holding Kai with a large smile on my face as I look down at him. I begin to click past it when Olive places her hand over mine on the mouse.

"I like this one," she says softly as she stares at the screen.

"Yeah." I look back at the photo. "Me too. Eddie insisted on taking it,"

We stare at the picture in silence for a few minutes when Olive finally speaks.

"I promise I'm trying to get there." She looks at me, her eyes full of the emotions she can't convey. "For the both of us."

Chapter 8

"Over and Over"
Olive

"I can't believe you went to talk to Laurie!" Ivy responds, mouth aghast, as she grabs two gowns out of an empty fitting room.

"Talk...technically no," I say, following her down the hallway to the storage racks in the middle of Vera Bridal. "See... yes. I didn't know if she would actually be there."

"And how many times have you done this?" Ivy asks, peering back at me as her pink heels clink across the tile flooring.

"Six...?" I answer sheepishly.

"SIX?" Ivy repeats, looking at me like I have smoke coming out of my ears. "And how long are you planning on doing this for?"

"Forever?" I squeak out.

"No, no, no." Ivy turns her whole body to face me now—she means business. "You need to either stop or talk to her."

"I can't."

"Why?"

I don't respond and Ivy raises an eyebrow.

"Why, Olive?" she repeats.

I blow out a breath before admitting to her, "I'm scared."

Ivy's expression softens from my confession. "I know you are." She takes the two sparkly gowns and places them on a rack.

"I feel like I can do many things," I tell her. "But... I don't feel like I can do this."

Ivy's posture relaxes some. "How did you even find out where she was staying?"

"I asked around," I say. "I asked Mr. Ray. I know she buys cigarettes from his store sometimes, or at least she always used to, and I was right. He still sees her almost weekly, he said."

"I'm sorry, but that's absolute bullshit that she buys cigarettes basically a block from your bar every week and consciously makes the decision to not even stop in."

"Are we surprised?" I respond. "It's always been like that for as long as I can remember."

"So why do you want to even try to talk to her? Why even waste your breath with the woman?"

"Because I need answers, and she's the only one that can give them to me."

"And what if she doesn't?" Ivy asks. "Are you prepared to deal with that?"

"I guess I will have to be," I answer with a shrug.

Ivy walks back up to the front of the shop and into another fitting room; I follow her, rushing to match her quick pace. For someone with legs half the length of mine, she sure moves quickly.

"What does Hunter think about all of this?" Ivy questions.

"He doesn't."

"He doesn't what?"

"He doesn't know," I admit.

Ivy spins to face me again. "What the fuck, Olive? Why

haven't you talked to your husband about this? If you're talking to me about this, he should know about it too."

"That's rich coming from you. There's obviously something you're hiding from me. I saw it in your face that night at Whiskey's. Even drunk you can't play that one off." I stare her down, refusing to let her brush it off with some quick change of subject again.

Ivy bites at her lower lip—she couldn't look more guilty right now if she possibly tried. "Fine," she states.

"Fine, what?" I reply.

"Come with me." She grabs my arm and yanks me down the hallway quickly before pulling me into the staff room.

"What are you doing?" I yelp out, and she turns and shuts the door behind me.

"I'm going to tell you something, and you have to swear to all secrecy that you aren't going to tell anyone."

"Okay." I nod.

"I mean it," she whispers. "Not. Even. Hunter."

"Wait, that's unfair. I don't even know what I'm agreeing to." I scoff. "You could tell me you committed murder."

"And you would rat me out to your husband just like that?" She snaps, and her voice raises an octave.

"You literally just lectured me about not telling him stuff!" I joke. "Did you commit a crime?"

"No!" she quickly replies. "Well... maybe? A crime of friendship."

Crossing my arms, I scold her. "Oh, god, Ivy. What did you do? You better tell me right now."

"Swear on Stefan and Damon Salvatore that you won't tell Hunter? He will find out eventually—I can promise you that. Even though this is absolutely the pot calling the kettle because you literally are hiding something from him right now about

Lauri—," Ivy rambles on, and I interject before her hair sets on fire.

"I swear. Just tell me."

"I'm kinda...married."

She looks at me, waiting for my response, but I can't give one; the only emotion I show in return is a blink.

"Did I break you?" Ivy asks, waving her hand in front of my face.

"What do you mean you're kinda married?" I repeat slowly.

Ivy opens her pink blazer and reaches down into the interior pocket before pulling a ring out and placing it on her wedding finger. "I mean, Donovan and I are married."

"I need to sit down," I whisper and walk over to the couch before plopping my body across it.

Ivy follows me, twisting her fingers against each other, obviously nervous by my response. "I'm sorry I didn't tell you before."

"When did you get married?" I sit up and wave my arms around the staff room. "I feel like I would remember if my best friend that owns a bridal store picked out a dress and went venue shopping, and I don't know... had a damn wedding?"

"Right before Christmas," Ivy says sheepishly, and I wince at the fact that that was almost seven months ago.

"Why didn't you tell me?" I can't hide the hurt from my tone. It's not like Ivy to keep something big like this from me.

She slides down on the purple suede couch next to me and breathes out deeply. "Well, it was spur of the moment for me too."

Ivy tells me a long story about how Donovan popped the question before Summer and Eddie's Christmas party and that they ended up eloping right then. Then, when they got to the party, ready and excited to tell everyone, Summer announced that she was pregnant with Kai, and they didn't want to steal her and Eddie's special moment.

"And so, it just kind of went on from there, and the longer it continued to be just between us, the *easier* it was to keep just between us."

"Your own little honeymoon phase," I answer, nodding my head in understanding.

"Exactly, I called it our love bubble." Ivy smiles sadly. "But, that's no excuse. I'm sorry I've kept it from you all these months. We are going to tell everyone else this year, I promise. We plan on doing a get together and telling everyone. I'm sure it will all work out fine and we will all celebrate as a group."

I can't hide the smirk that forms across my face, and Ivy eyes me strangely.

"What are you smiling like that about?" she asks, leaning away from me and closer towards the back of the couch with a nervous chuckle. "You look semi-evil right now."

"Oh, nothing. I just *knew* something was up with you. You can't get anything past me." I think for a moment and then add, "Well, at least for no longer than approximately seven months."

"Yeah, yeah, yeah." Ivy rolls her eyes. "You're smart and beautiful and whatever else I need to say to tell you that you're right," she jokes. "Now, if I can interject..."

"Please, don't," I tease, but she ignores me.

"You need to talk to your husband about Laurie."

"He doesn't know what she's like, though." I look down at my lap and hug myself with my arms slightly. "It's so embarrassing, and I really don't want him to see what she's like... especially now that she is the way she is." I turn my head to look at Ivy. "I don't want him to think of me differently."

"Babe," Ivy says, scooting closer to me and giving me a hug. "If you think your husband is going to judge you ever, then you don't realize how great the man you married is."

I begin to cry in my best friend's arms, feeling guilt wash over me in waves for the secret I've been keeping from my husband for the past few weeks. I wish this was never something that ran through my mind. I wish this situation with Laurie and my trauma from it were easier to explain.

Moments like this really make me miss Jane. I wish Jane could have met Hunter. I wish she could have loved him, too. I wish she were here to be my mom. But my wishes don't mean anything; it's nothing more than my hope waiting to be worthy enough to somehow come true.

Ivy runs her hands over my hair and lets me cry into her shoulder, mourning the mother that I never had and the one I did, but met too late.

Finally my tears slow, and I clear my throat.

"You're right," I tell her softly. "I'll talk to Hunter about it. Tonight."

Chapter 9

"The Good, The Bad, and The Ugly"
Olive

"Olive, are you almost ready to go?" I check the time on my phone before sliding it back into my pocket. It's past seven, and the Rinse and Repeat show has already started.

"Sorry, yes!" I hear the water shut off, and Olive opens the bathroom door. She's in a fitted black dress that stops at her thighs, and I'm instantly breathless as I take her appearance in.

"You look incredible, baby."

"Good enough to be your date, Curls?" She gives me a flirty wink as she steps past me and grabs a pair of black heels off the floor.

"Way out of my league," I tell her in response.

"You know I love you in green." She smiles, looking at my dark suit jacket with a white shirt under it.

"I feel like I'm going to work." I chuckle and touch my smoothed-back hair. "Who would have thought Rinse and Repeat would be playing a candlelit show at the community center?"

Isn't She Lovely

"Well," Olive states, finagling her right heel. "Even Wes the Mess can calm down his wild streak if it's for charity, right?"

"Yeah, you're right, and he really wants that skatepark to be approved. It's basically all he talks about now."

The concert tonight is being put on by the rec center with Wes's assistance. They are raising money for a new park that the town is going to build in the empty lot next to the center. Wes has been petitioning and talking to the mayor's office nonstop trying to make a skate park happen in that space since we've never had one on our side of Clairesville. Mayor Baker finally agreed with his plan, so tonight is a big deal.

"I mean, if anyone can raise the money, it has to be him. He's quite the showman." Olive slips on her second heel and then claps her hands together. "Let's go."

"You're right," I tell her, following her out of the room before taking her arm to help her down the steps. "Wes always puts on a good show."

As we walk down the staircase, Olive on my arm, we both spot the same thing at the exact same time.

Dog, our stubborn cat, is waiting by the front door, ready to block us from trying to leave.

"She knows we're departing," Olive whispers to me with a giggle.

"Yeah, as soon as she heard your heels clicking, I'm sure she knew something was up."

"Should we go out the side door? I don't want to hear a sad meow. My heart can't take it."

"Can you outrun her?" I joke. "She can do parkour across the walls before I can even finish blinking."

We get to the bottom of the stairs, and Dog walks over slowly, meowing at me. I feel like we are having a Wild West-style standoff with our nine-pound cat.

I reach down and rub my hand against the soft fur on the

top of her head. "Alright, Dog. Olive and I are going to leave for a little bit, but we'll be back soon."

"Very soon," Olive adds. "And look," she says, walking into the living room and grabbing the remote, holding it up to Dog like she's waving a white flag. "I'll even turn on Pet Paternity for you."

She starts up the TV, and Dog follows her cautiously into the room. Olive selects an episode with two owners fighting over who gets the custody of their alpaca in their messy divorce.

"Here," she tells our cat. "This is a good one; I just watched it last week. By the end of the episode, someone ends up shaved... but I won't say who. You have to watch for yourself, it's absolutely full of drama."

Dog looks at the TV and meows, seemingly pleased with Olive's pick of scheduled programming for her. She lies down on the carpet, and Olive raises her eyebrows at me, happy with herself, as she walks back over to me.

"Crisis averted," I say, kissing her dark hair.

"I didn't feel like getting scratched today; I just spent way too long shaving my legs for them to end up like Brillo Pads."

I look down at her legs, appreciating the long, smooth skin, getting momentarily distracted before Olive points at the door aggressively and then back at Dog.

"Let's go," I whisper, suppressing a chuckle, and we slowly back out of the front door before I shut it quietly behind us.

We get in my old pickup truck and Olive cranks on the radio before selecting an oldies station.

"Onward!" I call out as I back out of the driveway. "To watch Rinse and Repeat be classy and not..." I try to think of a word that rhymes, "trashy? For one show."

"Is that even possible?" Olive snorts.

"No. But for our sake and the sake of everyone in there with hundreds of candles, let's hope so."

Chapter 10

"Le Carnaval des Animaux, R. 125: VII"

Olive

The drive to the community center feels never-ending when I know I'm hiding something so monumental from my husband, when I should have just come out and said it from the start. I know he wouldn't be angry with me, but I also don't want to bring it up before the event tonight. I want to have one carefree night together before I have to deal with what this means with Laurie and finally verbalize to my husband why I'm trying to talk to her after all these years.

Right now, I just want to have fun.

Hunter's truck squeaks to a stop in the parking lot of the rec center, and it's shocking how many people are here. There have to be at least seventy cars in the lot, and with the plates being almost two hundred dollars per person, they must be raising some major funds for the park.

Once we make it to the front entrance, there's a teenager in a white shirt and bow tie waiting to open the door for us.

I thank him as we step inside, and Hunter leans in to whisper in my ear, "Hey, those uniforms look familiar. Did you lend him your old one?"

"Ha, ha," I deadpan. "I knew you were going to say that. You know I burned that thing as soon as I could."

"Understandable," Hunter responds.

We walk down the hallway for a moment longer, hearing soft classical music that grows louder as we stride to the end of the path with two solid white doors that lead us to the small gymnasium.

When Hunter pushes open the doors, we are suddenly surrounded by sounds and sights that I can only describe as magical. The whole space has been transformed into a glowing palace with white linens and greenery across every table. The only form of light in the room are the candles surrounding a small stage that Wes and the Rinse and Repeat boys stand on, playing classical music.

Beautifully.

"Holy shit," I say to Hunter. "Who is that up there?"

He is staring at the same spot as I am, watching Wes, mouth agape. Wes is in a full suit, with his facial hair completely shaved and his long blonde hair pulled back into a tight ponytail.

He actually looks like an elven leader.

"I'm shocked," Hunter sputters. "I have never seen him so…"

"Professional," I say, finishing his statement.

Hunter nods his head in agreement. "Come on," he takes my hand, "let's go find our seats."

We see a waiter in the back of the room, and he waves us over before guiding us to a round table across from a few other dressed-up couples. As we take our seats, I look around at the other couples, who all seem to be completely enthralled in the music as well.

Neither Hunter nor I do much but sip at our cocktails and nibble at our food while we continue to watch the band play in complete shock. I feel like Wes's body might have been invaded by an alien sometime earlier today. This is the guy we have to yell at three times on average during a Rinse and Repeat show at Whiskey Jane's for hanging from the rafters in the ceiling. Now here he is, playing Swan Lake with his eyes closed like some eighteenth-century composer.

Wes and the guys finish their final song of the night, and everyone stands to applaud for the band—calling out for an encore and cheering, while the mayor of Clairesville walks up to the microphone to close out the event.

"Thank you everyone for coming," Mayor Baker says, silencing the crowd. "I'd like to thank the boys from Rinse and Repeat for putting on such an amazing show for us all tonight. Let's hear it for the boys," he commands, and pauses while more applause rings out around the glowing room.

"Now please hush again everyone, I have a big announcement to make."

Wes makes eye contact with Hunter to my right and winks. This is it, the moment he announces the new park and skate park.

Mayor Baker continues, "We have been able to raise some large funds from this event, and I am now allowed to announce that this winter we will be breaking ground to build our very own pickleball court right here."

"Yeah!" Wes shouts with a cheer and causes Mayor Baker to jump in surprise from his spot at the microphone.

I cringe as I watch Wes seeming to actually process what was just said, and he repeats slowly, "Pickleball?"

"Yes," Mayor Baker answers with a chuckle. "We are so thrilled for this new addition to the community center."

Like watching a car crash about to happen, I can't turn away. Wes looks down at his suit, and his expression slowly turns to one of disgust as the mayor continues to talk.

"Uh-oh," I whisper into Hunter's ear.

"Not good," he agrees with me.

"So thank you everyone for coming, drive safe, and have a good night," Mayor Baker concludes, followed by applause from the audience. He steps off the stage, and I watch as Wes grabs the microphone back off the stand.

"Actually," Wes shouts, almost looking manic. "We want to play one more song for you guys. I heard you want an encore, right?" No one responds, so Wes repeats it again, even louder this time. "Right?!"

The crowd look around at each other, unsure what to do, and slowly people begin to sit back in their seats.

"Here we go, boys, let's play our favorite *classical* song," Wes yells into the microphone, his tone dripping with sarcasm and anger.

"I think we are about to witness a breakdown," I tell Hunter.

The band starts playing, and instantly I recognize the song "Killing In The Name by Rage Against The Machine."

Hunter looks at me and blows out a slow breath as he pulls his phone out of his pocket and hits record. "I think you're right."

Chapter 11
"I'd Love To Change The World"
Hunter

"I completely forgot how many times that song says 'fuck.'" Olive laughs from the passenger seat.

"I mean, Wes didn't *have* to rip off his shirt and throw it at Mayor Baker while flipping him off," I say with a chuckle. "But it *did* make for a good ending of the performance."

"Like I said, showman." Olive waves her fingers back and forth like spirit fingers. "He sure has 'it,' whatever *it* is."

"Razzle, dazzle," I joke.

"Yes, that's it," she replies sarcastically.

I reach over and take Olive's left hand before bringing it up to my lips and kissing the top of it. "Did you at least have a good night, babe?"

"It was great. One I'll never forget, that's for sure." Olive looks at me with a grin, but it doesn't seem to reach her eyes.

"What's wrong?" I ask, glancing away from her for a moment to look back at the road.

"We're almost home, can we talk once we get there?"

"Sure," I reply, but I can't help but feel worried.

We ride for the next few minutes in silence, and I rub the top of her hand with my thumb in comfort—I know more than anything, I'm trying to soothe my own nerves at this point.

Once I pull the truck into our driveway, I shut off the engine and immediately turn to face my wife. "Alright, we're home, now talk to me."

Olive unbuckles her seatbelt and slides closer to me, breathing out while she takes both my hands in hers.

"You're freaking me out," I tell her.

"Sorry, okay..." She looks down at my hands and blows out another quick breath. "I've been thinking about seeing my mom."

"Jane?" I ask, confused.

She looks up at me and shakes her head 'no' slowly. "My biological mother, Laurie."

I can't hide the shock that I know is currently plastered all over my face. Olive has shared quite a few things with me over the years that have caused me to have a strong distaste towards her birth mother.

"I know," Olive says, speaking quickly. "It's crazy."

"No, babe," I respond. "It's not crazy."

She looks back down at our joined hands. "I just feel like I need to get some answers about my childhood. I need to talk to her."

"Okay," I state, my mind made up to support my wife. "So how do we find her so you can have that conversation?"

"I kind of already have..." Olive replies sheepishly.

"You've visited her?"

She looks up and meets my eyes. "I've kind of been stalking her for the past few weeks."

"Babe." I blink in shock. "Where is she? Why didn't you tell me?"

"She's at the Jewel Mountain Motel," she replies and then

worries at her bottom lip with her teeth. "I don't know... Maybe because once you see my mom, you'll see the shame I hold about my upbringing. I didn't want to tell you because I didn't want you to judge me when you see what she's like."

"You can't help the family you were born into." I cup her chin with my hand tenderly. "I've told you this, I'm your family, I'll never disapprove of anything you tell me. You are not, your mo—Laurie. You're never going to be like her."

"Do you want to go to the motel with me when I go to talk to her?" Olive asks in a small voice.

"Yes."

"Tomorrow?" She looks up at me with her brown doe eyes.

I lean over to her seat and kiss her on the lips. "Yes."

Chapter 12
"There's Nothing Left for You"
Olive

Hunter and I stand outside the dingy motel room, and I feel his hand rub against the small of my back, comforting me, as I reach out and knock on the door three times.

The sound of footsteps shuffling from inside causes me to tense up, but this time, unlike the ones before, I stand resilient with my husband's presence and touch giving me the strength I need to stay grounded.

The door opens, and the small woman looking back at me doesn't even bat an eye at seeing me for the first time in fifteen years.

"So you're the one that's been leaving gifts on the doorstep, huh?" Laurie asks, and I watch as ash falls off the cigarette in her mouth onto the concrete walkway.

"Hi, Laurie," I reply, feeling the anger towards her begin to swirl around in my stomach.

"Who's the looker?" she says, pointing to Hunter with a cracked nail.

"This is my husband," I respond firmly. "Hunter."

"Hello, ma'am," Hunter politely says to her, and my mom completely ignores him.

"Well look at you, taking after me," she sneers. "Finding a nice tall man with a charming smile." She leans closer to me, and I can smell stale smoke and something minty on her breath as she whispers, like she's giving me some expert advice. "They all end up the same though."

I ignore her comment. "Laurie, I need to talk to you."

"Laurie." She snorts, obviously amused that I'm calling her by her first name instead of

Mom. "So talk."

I turn back to face Hunter, who still has his hand on my back protectively. "Will you give us a moment please, babe?"

Hunter looks down at me with a serious expression, and I can tell that he doesn't want to oblige, but he does anyway. "Sure, I'll be down in the truck if you need me."

He gives my mom a final serious look and then walks to the end of the concrete walkway before going down the steps. My mom's behavior is probably shocking to him—her brashness, her snappy tone—but to me this is the way it's been for a very long time.

She has always treated me like I'm an inconvenience that she never wanted but always had to be around. She's not known for her warm, inviting personality.

"So, what do you want to talk about?" Laurie asks, appearing bored by my presence on her doorstep. "I'm going to bingo in an hour."

"Why are you here, Laurie?"

She breathes out a harsh laugh. "You found me to ask me why I'm living in a motel?"

"No." I clear my throat and look around the unwelcoming balcony. "Can we sit down somewhere to talk? I'd feel better if I were sitting."

Laurie eyes me with a look of obvious exasperation. "Fine." She tosses her cigarette into the small ashtray outside of the door and steps back to let me in the small room. "Follow me."

As I step in, the smell of mold and old smoke permeates my nose, and the air almost feels wet as I breathe through my mouth to try and avoid the odor. There are crumpled-up food wrappers and crushed-up beer cans strewn out across a small two-person table. I feel a tightness in my chest as I look around the room; I wouldn't even wish this place or feeling on my enemies.

"You can sit on the bed," Laurie rasps out, taking a seat on the edge of the patterned quilt.

"It's okay," I say in a low voice. "I'll sit at the table."

Pulling out a chair, I see there's a pile of clothing in the seat —the clothing I've been dropping off for her each time I've stopped by. I lift it from the chair and place it on top of the trash. She didn't even bother to put on the things I left for her.

"Did you know it was me?" I ask, still looking at the new pairs of jeans, shirts, and sweatpants with tags on them.

"I had a feeling." Laurie grunts. "I think only you would drop off a care package for me. You always were making sure the house had stuff and asking me for money to get shit."

"I was hungry," I quiver, unable to hide the bite from my tone while still looking at the clothing. I can't bring myself to meet her eyes. "I was asking you for money to get groceries because the fridge was always empty."

"You never went hungry," Laurie responds lazily. "You always had what you needed."

"Yeah." I blow out a breath. "I guess that's true if you count out clothing that fits, a full stomach, and oh yeah..." I look up to meet her stare—I'm livid now. "Two parents that loved and cared for me."

"Oh, here we go." Laurie rolls her eyes. "Is this what you're here for? To tell me what a horrible mother I've been all these years? To seek your vengeance and hurt me since I did you so wrong in your head?"

"Hurt you?" I respond, unable to stop my voice from raising an octave. "If I were here to hurt you, why would I have left you clothes and money? I wanted to help you."

"I don't need your help," she barks back. "I've got a plan."

Things are escalating too quickly, and I breathe in deeply, trying to calm myself. Forcing myself to soften my tone, I ask, "Why are you here?"

Laurie smacks her hands against her thighs, irritated. "We got evicted. I'm waiting it out here."

"Who's we?"

"My boyfriend and I."

"And where's your boyfriend?" I question, already knowing where this is going. This whole routine is one I'm unfortunately familiar with.

"He had to leave town for a job, he'll be back," Laurie snaps —obviously feeling defensive with how it sounds, too. "I told you, I'm fine."

I don't even ask why she didn't go with him; I'm sure it was because he has to return to his wife or parole officer. My mom always dates the same type of men—emotionally and physically unavailable with a temper.

Why does she pick the men she does?

Thoughts of Hunter wash over me suddenly, and I feel a sense of pride in myself blooming. When I married him, I broke a cycle. Hunter's also right when he said I'm not like Laurie. I accept that now, and I'm not going to allow myself to stoop to her level and argue.

I glance down at my pants and trace the corduroy design with my index finger. "I saw you had a black eye the other day when I dropped off some stuff."

"Oh." My mom laughs, but it sounds more like a cough. "That was nothing; I fell down." She points her hand in my direction. "Don't spy on people. I taught you better than that."

Raising my head, I meet her eyes because she and I both know that I don't believe for a second that she fell. I don't even acknowledge her comment about "teaching me better" because there wasn't any parenting going on.

Breathing out slowly, I say, "I wanted to talk to you about being a... a parent."

"What? Did your boyfriend knock you up? You got a bun in the oven?" Laurie smiles and looks down at my stomach.

I can't even hide my annoyance. "My husband," I correct her. "And no. I haven't felt like I could have a child with my husband because I'm so worried about being a shitty parent like how I was raised." I stare deeply into her eyes as I continue, "I'm terrified of turning out like you. I don't want to do to a child what you did to me."

Instead of speaking, Laurie bursts out in a howl of laughter and doesn't stop.

"Is this funny to you?" I state as the anger is starting to bubble over now, and the cool resolve that I was trying to hold has quickly left my body. "You were a horrible parent."

Laurie wipes her eyes with the back of her hand from laughing so hard. "I wasn't a parent."

"Trust me, I know."

I start to stand up from the chair, unable to handle another moment of this ridicule. Who did I think I was going to be dealing with when I came to visit Laurie today? Did I really think she would be kind and give me some type of closure? Tell me I was a good person? That wouldn't be her nature.

"Sit, sit," she tells me and waves her hand in my direction.

Reluctantly, I do.

"I'm laughing," she explains as I stare at her. "Because I think it's hilarious that you think you would ever be like me."

"What are you talking about?" I spit out.

"I'm saying, you're nothing like me. I didn't want to be a mom; I never wanted to be a mom. So, I wasn't." She shrugs.

"But you," she continues. "You have always cared about people and stuck around for them. Look at how many chances you gave me as a kid. Look at how many times you had to be the 'parent'," she makes parentheses with her hands, "in our situation."

I sit in silence, the storm of anger still swirling violently around inside of me as I try to take in what she's saying.

"Have your kid." Laurie reaches across the bed and opens up her pack of cigarettes, pulling one out and placing it in her mouth. "You'll never be like me—you care too much," she adds with a look of disdain.

She says it like it's a bad thing.

As I glance around the room again, I feel something else surprisingly consume me. It's not disgust, or anger, or hurt—it's pity. I pity her for missing out on having a daughter like me. I pity that she will never get to see the woman that I am, how hard I work, and how loving of a wife I am. She's a sad person and I doubt I will ever get any of the answers that I'm looking for from her.

I begin to stand again, there's nothing else that needs to be said, she doesn't have the remedies for me, she'll never give me the closure I so craved.

My mom died years ago, and her name was Jane.

"I'm going to go," I say, walking myself to the door and opening it swiftly. The smell of fresh air whooshes into my face, and I feel like I can actually take a breath.

As I step out the door and onto the walkway, Laurie calls after me, "Olive."

I turn and look at the shell of the woman that gave birth to me.

Laurie shakes her head and gives me a small smile. "Now, don't think about me again after you leave here. I'm never going to change. You hear me? I'm not going to change. I'm set in my ways." She points in my direction with a suddenly serious expression. "You don't let me mess up your future like I already messed up your past."

Nodding my head in finality, "Goodbye, Laurie," and give her one last look before turning and walking down the steps.

For the first time in my life, with those final words from her, Laurie showed me she's actually capable of caring about me.

Chapter 13

"Goodbye Bread"

Hunter

As soon as I see Olive walking back down the steps, I straighten up in my seat. The ten minutes that she was talking to her mom felt like an eternity. All I wanted to do was go up there and tell her that she doesn't need validation from someone that can't even get their own life together, but I also know it's not my place.

This is her trauma, and my job as her partner is to support her through it.

She gets into the passenger seat, slamming the door, and then looks over at me. "Can we go?"

"Yes," I respond and turn my body to face backwards as I begin backing my truck out of the motel lot.

I'm almost relieved to see that her face isn't one with anger or streaked with tears, but I'm also unsure if I should ask her what happened immediately or wait. Olive has a habit of shutting people out when she's hurting—including me. She tends to process things in her head and then will open up after she thinks it through.

Music feels like a safe bet for now. I click on the radio, and we listen in silence for a few minutes as we drive back onto the main road.

"Wanna grab some food?" I ask, trying to lighten the mood.

"Only if it's Bricks," she says with a grin.

"Done." I U-turn my truck quickly, and Olive laughs as I gas the engine.

When her laughter finally dies down, her face is still smiling, so I reach out and squeeze her hand. "I'm proud of you, babe."

Olive nods her head. "You know what? I'm proud of myself too."

"Do you feel like you got some sort of closure?"

"Yeah," she responds, turning her head to look out her window. "Even though I didn't get what I wanted from her, I still got closure."

"How?"

"I realized that Laurie is weak, and she's always been that way. But I'm not. I'm solid, unbreakable, and I have been for a long time. I have the answers I've been craving, not Laurie."

My heart swells with pride in my wife as I bring her hand to my lips and kiss it gently. "You are *so* strong."

"And I think..." She stops speaking for a moment and seems to have an internal conversation with herself before continuing, "No, I *know* I will make a damn good mother."

"Yes you will, baby."

"And I'm going to be a mother on our time, on *our* terms. But I do want to have a child with you, Hunter. I love you so fucking much."

I know my friends rag on me all the time for being a sensitive guy, but I can't help it as tears of joy begin to fill my eyes.

Chapter 14

"Love and Happiness"
Olive

One month later

Hunter dries off from his shower and smiles at me before opening the drawer to pull out his boxers. I stare at his facial hair that he recently started to grow out into a beard, and I can't help but grin back—he looks rugged and sexy.

"No," I tell him. "Don't put them on; I want you."

He pushes his wet hair away from his face and raises an eyebrow at me. "Yes, ma'am."

I crawl towards the edge of the bed in nothing but a white tee-shirt, and Hunter meets me on the edge of the bed, completely nude.

Taking the sides of my face in his hands, he bends forward and begins to kiss me deeply. I feel his length harden against my stomach, and instantly a deep ache forms in my core to be filled with it.

I want him tonight, *all of him.*

Hunter lifts my tee-shirt over my head, exposing my naked

body. He gazes down at my breasts and slowly lowers his mouth to them, licking and teasing me delicately while never breaking our eye contact.

My legs feel shaky from the pleasure, and I lie back onto the soft, plush sheets while Hunter crawls back over me. I spread my legs wide for him, and he puts two fingers in me, smiling wickedly.

"So wet," he whispers to me, and I watch as he brings them to his mouth, tasting my desire for him on his tongue.

My head swims from the image of my husband licking my arousal off of his fingers. I feel so exposed, so turned on, so in love with this man.

He leans down over me and begins to kiss from my navel, up my chest, and finally stops at my neck. I feel his dick ready at my entrance. I try to push his weight down on me and I feel his penis tease my core ever so slightly.

"I want you," I moan into his mouth. "Now."

"Patience," he rasps out with a breathless laugh. "Good things take time." He loves to toy with me, dragging out my pleasure.

"Screw patience," I tell him.

The ache in my center is enough to drive me insane, and I want to be filled with him this second. I thrust my hips upward towards him, sinking his dick inside of me. Hunter instantly lets out a hiss of pleasure.

"Fuck," he moans deeply.

God, I love a man that moans.

He leans down and kisses me, swirling his tongue in my mouth and fucking me at the same time. I grab onto his hair with both hands and tug slightly, trying to somehow press him even closer towards me. Nothing makes me feel more connected to him than when our bodies twist and dance together in bed, speaking a secret language that only the two of us know.

Hunter draws out of me slowly before plunging back inside, and I yell out in pleasure. He leans down and rasps against my ear, "You feel so fucking good."

I throw my head back onto the pillow, moaning. I let go of his hair and grab onto the sheets with both hands as he continues to talk to me, whispering sweet nothings while he thrusts into me.

"You're driving me insane, Olive."

I feel the fire building in my core, and he begins to tense above me; I can tell he's getting close, too.

He bends down and kisses me again, tasting my tongue, panting into my mouth.

"Hunter," I say, drawing back from his lips slightly. "I'm ready."

"Okay, I'm close too," he responds—he's not understanding what I'm saying.

"No," I tell him, looking up into his dark brown eyes, and he stops moving above me. "I'm *ready*. I want to have a baby with you."

Hunter's face morphs into one full of emotion. "You mean it?"

"Yes." I shake my head quickly as my chest heaves wildly.

He bends down and plants his lips back on mine, kissing me with an intensity that I didn't even know was possible.

"I love you, I fucking love you so much," he says as he thrusts into me, never breaking our eye contact.

My pussy begins to spasm, and I grab onto Hunter's back, raking my fingers down it as I finish. Hunter watches me ride out my orgasm, his eyes dark with desire as my face contorts from the pleasure.

"I can't hold back any longer, babe," Hunter moans animalistically, and I feel him release inside of me.

When he finishes, we are both breathing heavily from absolute satisfaction, and Hunter collapses onto the bed next to me. Before I can even smile, his lips are back on mine. "I love you."

We are really doing this; we're going to be parents together someday.

Chapter 15

"Comin Home Baby"

Hunter

One month later

"And I'd like to thank Hunter Rowe, owner of Rowe Records and our videographer for the night. Hannah and I couldn't have asked for a better person to film our special day." The groom, Anthony, smiles at me, holding up his glass of champagne in one hand and the microphone in the other.

I tilt my head down in thanks, still behind the camera while he continues to give his thank-you speech at the vastly extravagant reception. "You've been a blast to work with, and I'm sure the boys will be waiting anxiously for another round of skate with you."

The row of groomsmen to his left all laugh in unison, and I chuckle behind the camera. I've been in Cabo with them to film their whole trip of nonstop partying for the past four days leading up to the wedding. I feel like I practically know the group like family at this point.

That's one of the fun things about filming big moments like

this; I still get to travel and do all the things I love, like experiencing new places and meeting new people.

Anthony closes out his speech, and I pan the camera to the room of guests all applauding him. The DJ plays a foghorn sound, and the lights dim significantly as a disco ball lowers from the top of the ballroom ceiling as booming bass sounds out.

This is the part where my job really begins—when the dance floor opens and the drinks start double pouring.

Checking the camera, I make sure my battery is ready to go —fully charged, good. I look up just in time to press record and capture the bride riding on her maid of honor's back across the dance floor.

* * *

I'm standing in line at the airport convenience store with a magazine and a water bottle when my phone rings loudly in my back pocket. Pulling it out, I smile when I see the caller ID, Olive.

"Hey babe," I say, answering the phone. "You caught me just in time; I'm going to be boarding soon."

"I can't wait to see you," she breathes out on the other side of the call.

"You sound wide awake for it being seven in the morning." I laugh. Olive is not known to be a morning person since she usually works late at the bar.

"Yeah, I couldn't sleep. I just felt restless, and I miss you. It's hard to sleep when you're away."

"I know; I'll be home soon."

She's quiet on the other side of the line.

"You okay?" I question.

"Fuck it," she exclaims. "I can't wait any longer. I'm pregnant!"

"What?!" I shout, dropping the magazine and water on the floor, and definitely scaring the woman behind me in line. "Sorry," I mouth to the lady and step out of the line, grabbing the items off the floor.

"Yes," Olive responds, laughing with joy. God, I love her laugh. I wish I could wrap her in my arms and give her a kiss right now.

"I can't believe it." I look around at my surroundings, wishing I was with her right now. "We're having a baby."

"We're having a baby," Olive repeats. "Now get home to me safe. We have a lot to figure out."

"I'll be home soon. I love you."

"I love you too, Curls," she tells me before ending the call.

Breathing out deeply, I take in the moment, the moment I just found out I'm going to be a dad. I wonder if this is how my own father felt when he found out about me.

The sound of my gate being called plays over the airport intercom, and I look at the items in my hand, realizing I still need to go pay.

As I walk over to get back in the line of customers, something catches my eye to the left in the shop. I stride over and look at the baby onesie with the word "Cabo" across it in bright yellow letters and take the hanger off the rack.

My first gift for my child.

Chapter 16

"To Build A Home"
Olive

8 months later

"One more push, Olive," Hunter tells me, cheering me on. "You're almost there."

"We can see the baby's head," my OBGYN encourages me. "Just a few more seconds—you're almost there."

I take a deep breath in and then exhale and push as hard as I can, using all of my force and will to focus on the moment. My frustration, my difficult pregnancy, and my heartbreak in the past—I get it all out with one final push. This is my moment of power. My moment of triumph—

I hear a cry.

"Olive," Hunter chokes out, emotion lacing every word as he reaches over to grab my hand. "It's a girl."

My moment that motherhood begins.

Chapter 17

"Home"

Hunter

"Alright," Johnny says, pushing through the doorway of our hospital room. "Let's see this little bugger."

"Slow it down." Rick laughs from next to him with a large bouquet of flowers in one hand and a little gift box in the other one. "You're going to scare the baby, Johnny. No one wants to hear your squawking this early."

"Oh shut it, you old geezer," Johnny answers. "Kids love me."

"I see that Tweedle Dee and Tweedle Dum have arrived," Mrs. Sonjia quietly jokes, glancing up from my newborn baby that she's currently rocking in her arms.

Rick notices first that Olive is asleep just as I hold a finger over my mouth before nudging my head in the direction of her in the hospital bed. She had a long night of figuring out how to nurse our little girl. It's not as easy as people tell you, we learned.

Our little girl, I think to myself.

When I found out it was a girl yesterday, I was thrilled. I

never told Olive I had a preference since she told me she wanted to wait to find out the gender of the baby till she gave birth, but I really wanted a little girl.

The only thing better than one Olive is two. Now I have a little version of my wife with fair skin and big doe eyes. Husband has always been my favorite title, but that will have to share the top spot with Father now.

Rick gives Mrs. Sonjia and me a large grin as I accept the gift and bouquet from his hands. "Thank you. Olive's gonna be so bummed if she slept through you guys visiting." I get ready to stand and go over to her, but Mrs. Sonjia reaches out her hand and shakes her head gently.

"Maybe don't wake her," she tells me. "The poor thing is exhausted."

"Yeah," Johnny adds, eyes wide with a haunted expression. "Rob told us she was in labor for thirty-two hours." He pretends to shiver. "I don't wish that on my worst enemy."

I look over at my wife, feeling pride for her strength blooming inside of me. "She did it. She never showed an ounce of fear the whole time." Even though I know she *was* afraid.

"A little girl," Rick whispers, looking down at my child. "She's going to have a lot of people to protect her and look out for her, huh?" He chuckles.

"I'm sure it will drive her insane," I agree with a laugh. "There will be too many eyes watching out for her in town when she's a teenager."

Johnny chuckles, and Rick nods his head. "You've got that right."

"Do you guys want to hold her?" I ask.

"No, no, she looks content in Sonjia's arms. We will get out of your hair now," Rick responds. "I don't want to wake Olive—we just wanted to drop off this stuff and say congrats to you guys."

"Make sure Olive opens the gift when she wakes up," Johnny pipes up. "That one's from me."

Well, this will be interesting.

"Okay," I promise him. "I will."

Rick turns and points at the whiteboard behind us with our daughter's time of birth and weight.

"Is that her name?" he asks and then clears his throat.

"Yes," I respond. "Olive let me pick it."

"Great choice," Rick says. "Call me once you guys get back home, and we will stop by with some pizza."

"Thanks, guys," I tell them, grateful for the support from Olive's chosen family.

Johnny reaches over and pats me on the back. "Try to get some shut-eye too, barstool boy. I see those bags."

I chuckle at the nickname.

They both leave the room, and Mrs. Sonjia smiles at me. "I'm going to head out too; I'll give you guys some time alone, just you three... Well, until the nurses come back in every thirty minutes," she teases.

She and I were running a tab on a sheet of paper yesterday about how many times someone would come in within the hour. We were up to nine times before we gave up on keeping score, deciding it was enough.

Mrs. Sonjia hands my daughter to me gently and stands. Her long skirt swishes around her ankles as she walks over to Olive and softly places a kiss on the top of her head before walking out.

* * *

"I've got to say, hospital food isn't that bad." Olive takes a giant bite out of the club sandwich in front of her with a large platter of fries. "I'm also ravenous, so maybe I'm a bad judge of that right now."

I push my plate towards her. "I think my meatloaf just moved. You're definitely biased from burning so many calories nursing."

Olive shrugs and shoves a fry dipped in ketchup into her mouth. "I mean, your first mistake was ordering meatloaf."

"I'm not taking this meatloaf slander," I tease her. "You just need to try it. Meatloaf is delicious."

"Well, now's not the day to start." Olive snorts. "You literally just said it's moving."

"Touché," I say, looking at my plate in moderate disgust. I don't think it's supposed to be wet and dry at the same time.

Olive looks over at the corner of the room to where the flowers from Rick are resting, and I realize I never gave her the gift from Johnny.

"One second," I tell her, standing quickly and grabbing the small square box out from behind the flowers. "I forgot to give you this. Johnny said *you* have to open it. I was not allowed." I laugh.

Olive raises an eyebrow. "Nothing better pop out at me or I might scream." We both look over at our girl sleeping in the hospital bassinet.

"It should be fine. We both know he can have his serious moments; maybe it's just a nice pair of mittens or a card."

"Mittens... right," Olive says sarcastically. "Sounds like a gift he would get."

I hand her the box. "Only one way to find out."

She rests the present in her lap and begins to open it slowly, peeking into the box to make sure nothing is spring activated. Obviously relieved that nothing happened, she opens it the rest of the way, and as she looks down, she bursts into tears.

"What?" I ask, worried.

Isn't She Lovely

Olive shakes her hands quickly back and forth and continues to bawl, slowly lifting something out of the package.

When I see what it is, I stifle a laugh. It's the smallest little black top hat that I've ever seen in my life.

"Look at this," Olive states through tears. "She'll be like a tiny Johnny."

Chapter 18

"Je Te Laisserai Des Mots"

Olive

The drive home from the hospital feels surreal. What do you mean you just give birth and leave, and now this little perfect child is mine to raise and care for...? Where do I even begin?

It feels uncanny that you walk into the hospital as a family of two and walk out as a family of three a few days later. Hunter and I looked at each other once we got in the car and immediately began to laugh because we both felt the exact same way—this is insane.

As if he can feel that I'm thinking about him, Hunter glances back at me in the rearview mirror and winks at me. "How are you doing back there, Mom?"

I reach over and squeeze our daughter's tiny hand in the car seat next to me. "I'm doing fantastic. I haven't cried in the past..." I look at the clock. "Fifteen minutes," I deadpan.

These damn postpartum hormones—they are worse than the pregnancy ones, I swear. When we got in the car and the music started up, it was playing some slow song that was on the radio, and I just burst into tears for no reason. Hunter shut it off immediately and switched it to a Limp Bizkit CD in the player.

Limp Bizkit isn't tear provoking.

We turn off of the main road onto a side street, and I look at Hunter in the mirror again, confused this time.

"Where are we going?"

"I thought you would want to make a quick stop first before we go home."

I look out the window and stare at the canopies of trees and neighborhoods as we pass. I know exactly where we are going now.

Answering softly, I tell him, "You read my mind."

We curve along the narrow tree-lined road between neighborhoods until we reach a clearing that I've become very familiar with.

Hunter pulls my SUV into the gravel lot and parks by the gate entrance. "Do you want me to go with you two?" he asks.

"Would you be upset if I said I want to go alone this time?"

"Absolutely not," Hunter answers. "Let me help you guys get out."

He steps out of the driver's side and opens my door behind him, giving me his hand to help me step down. Then he reaches around me and begins to gently lift our daughter out of her car seat.

"You okay to walk with her over there alone?" Hunter asks, worry in his tone.

"Yeah." I nod. "I'm actually feeling really good right now."

"Good," he replies, handing her off to me and kissing me on the top of the head gently. "I'll be here if you need me."

"Thanks, curls." I grin at him before turning towards the gate and walking through the opening.

My sneakers crunch down on the gravel path, and I cut off

to the right, following the worn-down trail in the grass before stopping at my destination.

I sit down slowly in the grass, holding my child tight, and breathe out.

"Hi, Mom," my voice quivers as I look up at the gravestone that reads Jane Fern. "I wanted to introduce you to your granddaughter. Her name is Jane Lily Rowe."

Turning baby Jane, who is swaddled tightly in my arms, I watch as she opens her eyes. It's like she senses that this moment is something significant. Grinning down at my daughter, I feel a warmth and comfort wash over me. A moment of peace, like my mother Jane is somehow here with me too.

I look down at my daughter in awe and whisper, "Isn't she lovely?"

Acknowledgments

First, to my readers, thank you for reading Olive and Hunter's continued love story. I will always appreciate you taking the time to read one of my novels, and your support in my work means everything to me.

Second, thank you to my beta readers: Breanna, Kasie, Jesse, Crystal, Katie, and Edith. All of your feedback and attention to Olive and Hunter's journey have helped tremendously. I'm so grateful for you all!

Thank you to Rattle The Stars PR for being amazing as always. Jess and Heather, you are the sweetest and work your butts off for your authors. Heather, thank you for editing Isn't She Lovely and for all your amazing feedback. Thank you for answering my texts about edits no matter what time of day, also LOL.

Thank you to Jesse for proofreading the novel. I so appreciate your great eye and friendship!

Thank you to my street team; I've loved getting to know you guys and want to give you all giant hugs. I hope to meet each and every one of you in person some day!

To my Jane Doe's, I love you guys so much and will always be so grateful for your friendships and hype. I am so lucky to have day one girls like you guys!

To Jordan, Gwen, Ollie, and Rowan, I love you guys more than I can put into words, and that's saying a lot since I'm an author. (lol) I get to live my own fairy tale with you guys by my side every day.

To all my family and friends that have supported me in one way or another, I see you, and I love you. Thank you all.

Keep reading for a sneak peek
at Book 3 in the Claireville series

Just What I Needed

"No More Tears"
Dove

Eighteen Years Ago

Watching my mom walk up and down her row of customers, I slouch farther down into the worn blue booth. I *hate* days when Marv isn't working; that means no free apple pie or vanilla ice cream with a sprinkle of cinnamon on top for me.

My stomach growls.

Last Sunday, he surprised me by letting me hangout in the kitchen and watch the guys make croissants and pancakes during my mom's whole morning shift—I even got to flip a few of my own. They turned out burnt and lumpy, but Marv bit into one anyways and said it was "absolutely delicious" and that I "have a gift."

Mrs. Werther is managing today, and she won't even let me take a few lemon slices and sugar to add to my water in attempts to make lemonade.

So, today blows.

My mom glances over her shoulder at me with a worried expression, and I make sure to give her a quick smile before

"No More Tears"

turning back to the napkin covered in ink in front of me. I'm currently scribbling cute monsters on with one of the office pens—another thing Mrs. Werther would be upset about. I can hear her in my head now.

"*Dove Ann! You know that costs The Looney Spoon a cent every time you take something. Do you want us to close down and your mom to not have a job?*"

I wanna tell that lady where she can put her job and it's one of the bad words I heard from my mom arguing with my dad on the phone.

Today's drawing is a bubble monster with googly eyes and black spikes for armor. Every single monster I draw always has to have some black, it's my favorite color. My older sister Darla always picks on me about it, saying that black isn't a real color and its *weird* for an eight year old to like black—that just makes me like it more.

Once the picture is complete, I shove it in the front zipper pocket of my backpack where it's already bursting with other napkin doodles from previous days. Then, I unzip the large pocket with my brother's white iPod that I stole without him noticing this morning and two baking magazines that Marv left for me.

Grabbing the top magazine with a stacked cake covered in bright green frosting on the cover, I set it on the table in front of me and pull out Dino's iPod, too. I glance around to make sure no one is looking and then turn it on.

He would be livid if he knew I took it. He saved up all of his birthday and Christmas money to buy it, but sometimes I am able to "borrow it" without him noticing. I'm hoping that's how today goes too.

Moving my thumb across the circle in the center of the white iPod, I scroll through the songs. I'm looking for the band

"No More Tears"

I've been listening to every time I borrow it—I think I have the same taste in music as my brother.

Placing the headphones in my ears, "No More Tears" by Black Sabbath starts to play and I turn the volume up all the way, bobbing my head to the beat as I absorb pages and pages of baking tips and recipes. I dog ear a few pages that I want to try and make this weekend if my mom lets me use the oven.

By the time I finish reading the magazine, it's still been only forty-five minutes, and I'm SO bored. Glancing out the window near the booth, I watch kids ride by on their bikes and wish I could be outside too.

Today is the first day in months that it hasn't been freezing, and I really want to go outdoors. My teacher this year is such a grump at school that we barely get recess.

Maybe... just for a minute.

Looking around from the corner of the booth, I see my mom busy with a large round booth of six guests. Perfect, I can make my escape while she's distracted and if I leave my backpack she will probably just think I'm in the bathroom. I glance around for Mrs. Werther's judging gaze next and see her behind the diner counter, talking to one of the regulars.

It's now or never.

I grab Dino's iPod and headphones before rapidly slinking out of the booth while still facing my mom. I make sure she doesn't turn my direction and notice me as I slowly go through the kitchen doors.

Thankfully, she doesn't even look my way once, and I silently cheer to myself as I quickly breeze by the cooks. None of them even glancing in my direction since the dinner rush has started.

Once I push through the backdoor of the kitchen I do a quick look around, and when I see there's no staff out back, I silently cheer. I think I just successfully escaped from Mrs.

Werther's prison. I breathe in a deep gust of fresh air and release it slowly.

Sweet victory.

I start to take off in a jog since I know my time is limited, and decide to go to the park a block away. At least I will be able to do the swings for a few minutes there.

I love swinging. It makes me feel weightless and free, far away from the stress and worry that I constantly feel at home. My stomach always hurts when my mom gets upset with stuff my dad says to her on their weekly phone calls. My older sister told me it's anxiety.

I'm not sure what that means, but I hope it goes away soon.

When I make it to the wooded park next to the little run-down pond, I'm excited to see there's no one here. I get the swings all to myself.

Putting the headphones back in my ears, I choose the farthest swing to the left of the playground and start to do the familiar pump back and forth motion with my legs and torso to start my momentum.

Another Black Sabbath song plays, and I sing out the lyrics, not caring if I'm loud since I'm alone except for the ducks and geese at the pond. My mood lifts more and more by the second, I love this feeling.

One song after another continues to play, and I'm out of breath by the time I slow to a stop, not only feeling a new lightness in my head, but also off my shoulders. My black converse drag against the gravel as I sit still for a moment and look around at the playground in front of me.

Suddenly, I feel a sharp pain on the back of my ankle and cry out in shock.

What the?

Terrified, I turned to see a goose directly behind me, and yank the headphones out of my ears while jumping up quickly from the swing. The goose is hissing at me, something I didn't even know they could do, and waddling a step closer to me.

I back up a step, the goose follows me getting closer again.

I panic.

I start running as fast as my legs will carry me, which isn't that fast, I realize—I'm not a very active kid. I begin yelling out for "help" asking for someone to save me but no one is around. Now I regret being happy about the park being unoccupied.

Glancing behind me as I run, I see the goose following closely with its wings splayed widely as it continues to hiss and honk at me. As I face forward again, whimpering in fear, I trip suddenly on a raised piece of old concrete on the sidewalk.

When I hit the pavement, I try to catch my fall but I'm not quick enough and I can feel my knee drag across the ground. I look down at my pants and see a large rip across my new black jeans that I had begged my mom for a few weeks ago.

I'm going to be in so much trouble.

Bright red blood is starting to drip from my skinned knee, and I notice my converse are untied on the left, which is what must have caused me to trip so badly when I hit the bump in the sidewalk.

Hearing another aggressive honk, I look up to see that the goose keeps getting closer and closer, it's only a few feet from me now. I begin to accept my fate that I'm about to be geese food, until suddenly, I hear the roar of an engine.

Looking up, I see a person on a red dirt bike quickly pulling up next to me. The engine has a deep rumble and the driver revs some kind of gear on the handlebar that causes a loud noise that instantly seems to spook the goose. It honks a final time before quickly backing up and flying off towards the pond.

I watch it, still breathing heavily when I hear the dirt bike driver ask me a question.

"No More Tears"

"Are you okay?" a muffled male voice asks me through his black dirt bike helmet.

Turning to peer back at him, I feel embarrassed and quickly stand up and brush off my pants. I can't really make out his face from the helmet, but he is probably a high schooler like my brother—they sound similar and this boy looks about the same size.

"Yeah, I'm fine." I look over the dirt bike taking in the cherry-red color and then advert my eyes feeling more nervous now that the adrenaline has left me.

"Your knee is bleeding a little," the teenager tells me in a kind voice and motions to my leg.

If possible, I'm even *more* embarrassed now that he has noticed how clumsy I am. This kid is obviously cool. He has a dirt bike that he gets to ride around for fun, and all I have is a skinned knee and a backpack full of napkin drawings.

Crap, napkin drawings.

I need to get back to The Looney Spoon immediately—my mom will be so mad at me if she finds out I left the restaurant. I've been gone way longer than I should have.

Not knowing what else to say in my sudden panic and humiliation, I turn and start to run away back towards the direction of the restaurant. The guy calls out from behind me, saying something else but I don't even try to listen to what he's saying or glance back.

Whoever he was, he was a stranger, another thing that I would get scolded for. My mom is constantly telling me stories about how men love to lure kids into their cars with promises of candy or puppies. That teenager could have easily scooped me up onto his dirt bike and sped off with me.

Maybe I would like to be somewhere else.

Running as quickly as I can down the pavement, one of my shoes catches on the other one and I glance down and remember I didn't tie it after I fell. I bend down and make a quick bow before double knotting it—I only have half a street left until I'm back at The Looney Spoon.

I think I will be able to make it inside without anyone noticing.

When I finally see the restaurant, I duck behind the nearby trees and go around back, slamming to a halt when I see my mom looking hurriedly around the employee parking lot near the dumpster.

Well, crap again.

I breathe out and know I need to put her worries to bed. I call out to her. "Mom, I'm here."

She quickly turns to face me. "Baby! I was worried sick about you." She approaches me faster than I can get to her and yanks me into her arms. "Where the hell have you been?"

"I just went on a walk," I lie. A walk would probably get me in less trouble then saying I went to the park, got attacked by a goose, and then talked to a boy on a dirt bike.

"You know I would never allow you to walk alone!" my mother snaps. "There are men with vans—"

"Yes, I know. The candy," I tell her. "Sorry," I add, but don't really mean it.

I'm sick of being stuck at the restaurant every day after school; I don't get why I can't stay at the apartment with Darla or go wherever Dino goes. I'm the only one that is treated like a baby.

"Exactly, and puppies." She lets go of me and steps back, crossing her arms in frustration while giving me a once-over. I cringe as she looks down at my black jeans and does a double take when she sees my knee. I watch as her expression turns even more sour. "And I see you ruined your new pants?"

"Sorry," I apologize again before looking down.

The feeling of shame consumes me. I really do mean the

sorry this time, I know my mom has to work hard to save up to buy us new things. These jeans cost almost thirty dollars. My mom didn't want to buy them, but I had begged her for them.

"I'll still wear them," I tell her. "I kind of like the hole, it's cool."

My mother lets out an exasperated breath before waving me on. "Come on, we need to get back inside. Mrs. Werther doesn't need any excuses to dock my hours or even worse, not allow you to be here with me."

Nodding my head, I follow my mom back inside for the remainder of her shift.

It's not until that night that I realize I made the biggest mistake of all when my older brother barges into the room that I share with Darla and asks me where his iPod is.

I say my first bad word. "Shit."

About the Author

Nicole Mikell lives in sunny Florida with her husband, three kids, and two dogs. When she's not busy reading, you can find her thrift shopping or watching K-pop music videos with her daughter. Nicole loves reality TV, anything artsy, and a good Youtube dance workout.

She also really loves music, so send her some song suggestions.

You can follow her for future book updates on Instagram and TikTok:

Instagram: @nicolemikellauthor
Tiktok: @authornicolemikell

Also by Nicole Mikell

Baby, It's You
You Can't Hurry Love
Isn't She Lovely

www.ingramcontent.com/pod-product-compliance
Lightning Source LLC
LaVergne TN
LVHW030324070526
838199LV00069B/6550